W9-BZQ-056

DISCARDED
from the Nashville Public Library

NPLF

Nashville Public Library | FOUNDATION

*This book given
to the Nashville Public Library
through the generosity of the*
**Dollar General
Literacy Foundation**

NPLF.ORG

THERE WAS AN OLD LADY WHO SWALLOWED A SHELL!

by Lucille Colandro
Illustrated by Jared Lee

SCHOLASTIC INC.

New York   Toronto   London   Auckland   Sydney
Mexico City   New Delhi   Hong Kong   Buenos Aires

NASHVILLE PUBLIC LIBRARY

With love to Aunt Grace and Aunt Connie
— L.C.

To my daughter, Jennifer, who brightens my day
— J.L.

No part of this publication may be reproduced, stored in a retrieval system, or transmitted in any form or by any means, electronic, mechanical, photocopying, recording, or otherwise, without written permission of the publisher. For information regarding permission, write to Scholastic Inc., Attention: Permissions Department, 557 Broadway, New York, NY 10012.

ISBN-13: 978-0-439-87380-2
ISBN-10: 0-439-87380-0

Text copyright © 2006 by Lucille Santarelli.
Illustrations copyright © 2006 by Jared D. Lee Studio, Inc.
All rights reserved. Published by Scholastic Inc.
SCHOLASTIC, CARTWHEEL BOOKS, and associated logos are trademarks and/or registered trademarks of Scholastic Inc.

30 29   15/0

Printed in the U.S.A.
This edition first printing, April 2008

There was an old lady who swallowed a shell.
I don't know why she swallowed the shell.
She didn't tell.

There was an old lady who swallowed a crab.
Why did she grab that crawling crab?

She swallowed the crab to live in the shell.
I don't know why she swallowed the shell.
She didn't tell.

There was an old lady who swallowed a fish.

What a tickly dish, that swimming fish!

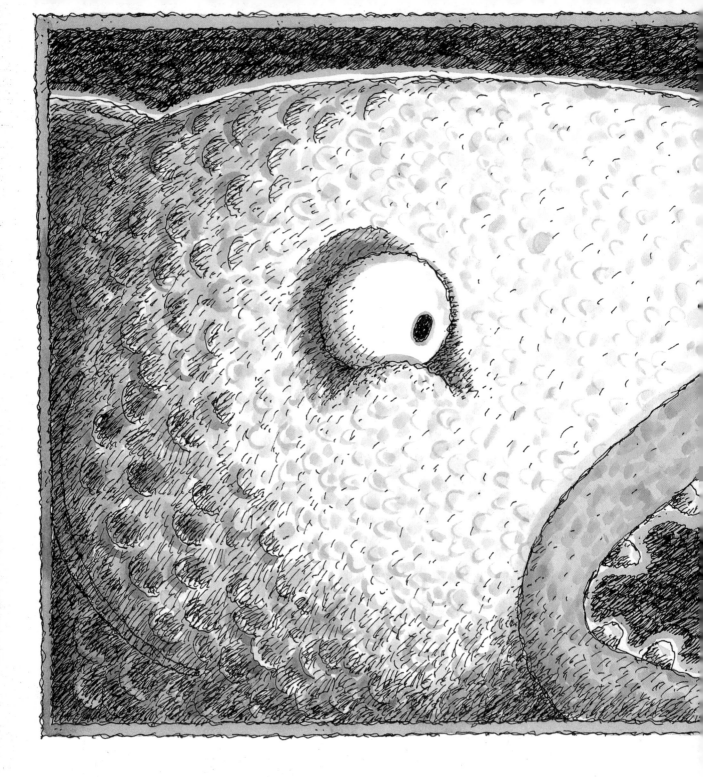

She swallowed the fish to catch the crab.
She swallowed the crab to live in the shell.

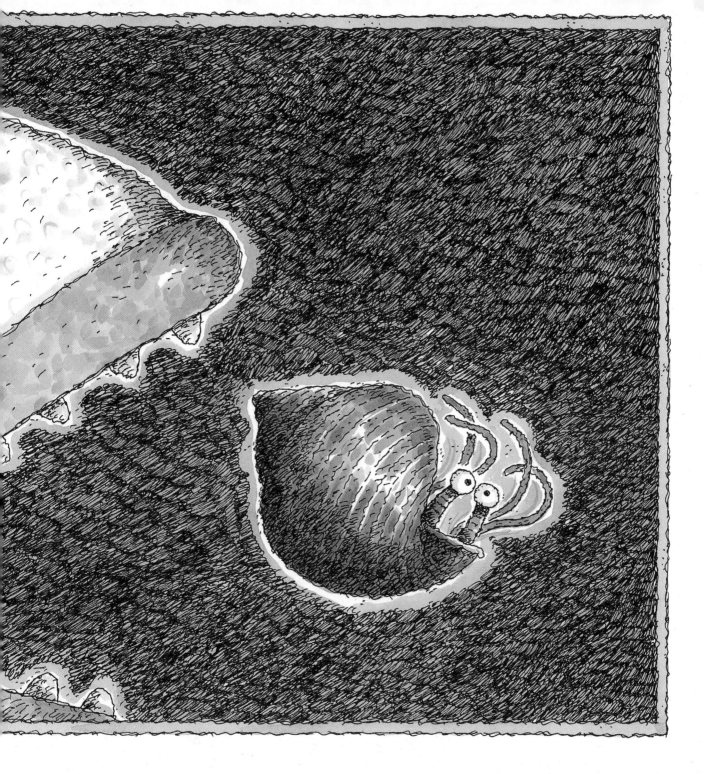

I don't know why she swallowed the shell.
She didn't tell.

There was an old lady who swallowed a gull.

It wasn't dull to swallow a gull.

She swallowed the gull to scoop up the fish.
She swallowed the fish to catch the crab.
She swallowed the crab to live in the shell.

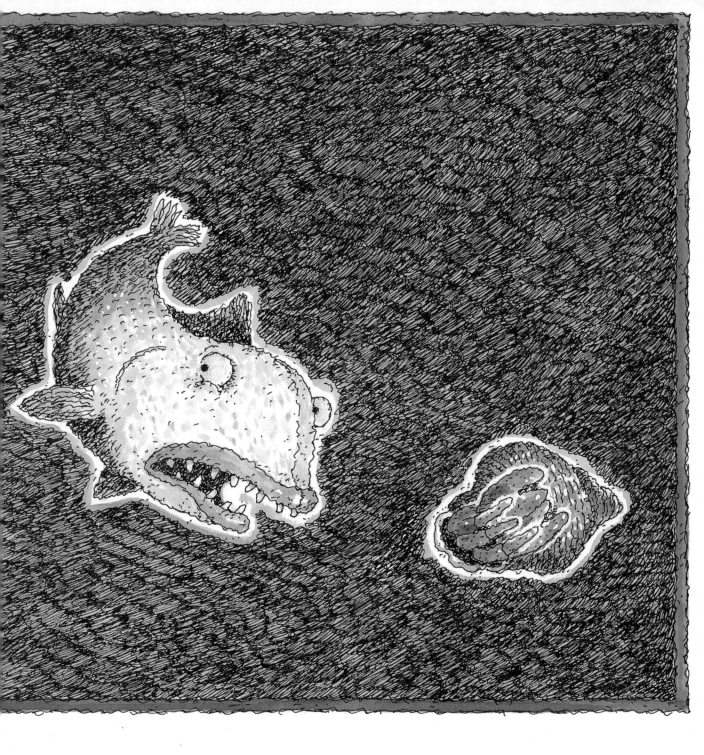

I don't know why she swallowed the shell.
She didn't tell.

There was an old lady who swallowed a pail.

She didn't wail when she swallowed the pail.

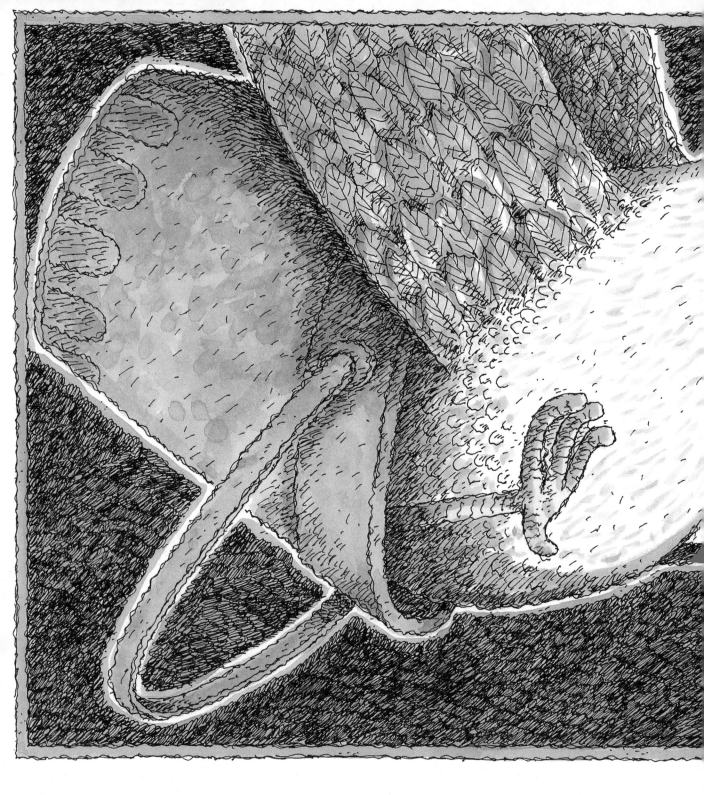

She swallowed the pail to carry the gull.

She swallowed the gull to scoop up the fish.

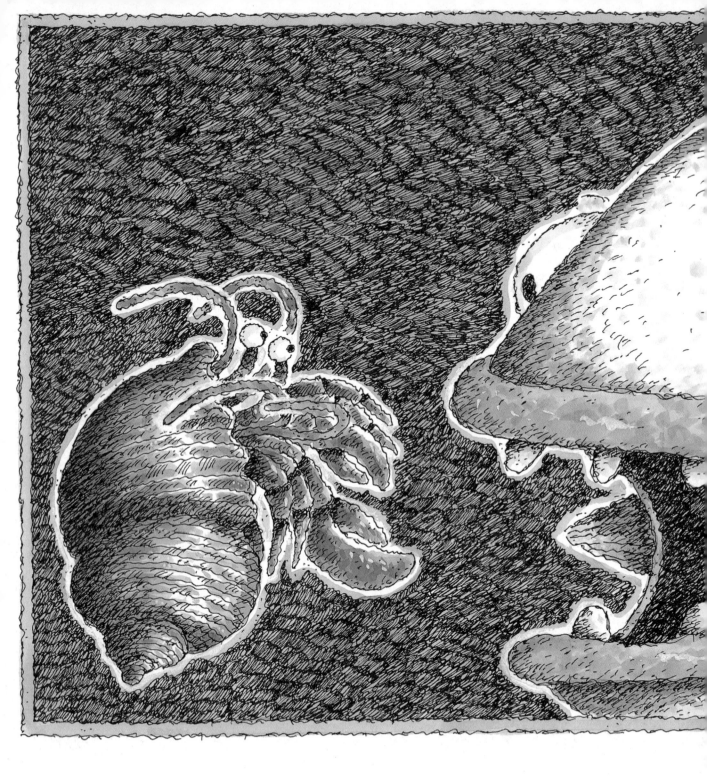

She swallowed the fish to catch the crab.
She swallowed the crab to live in the shell.

I don't know why she swallowed the shell.
She didn't tell.

There was an old lady who swallowed some sand.

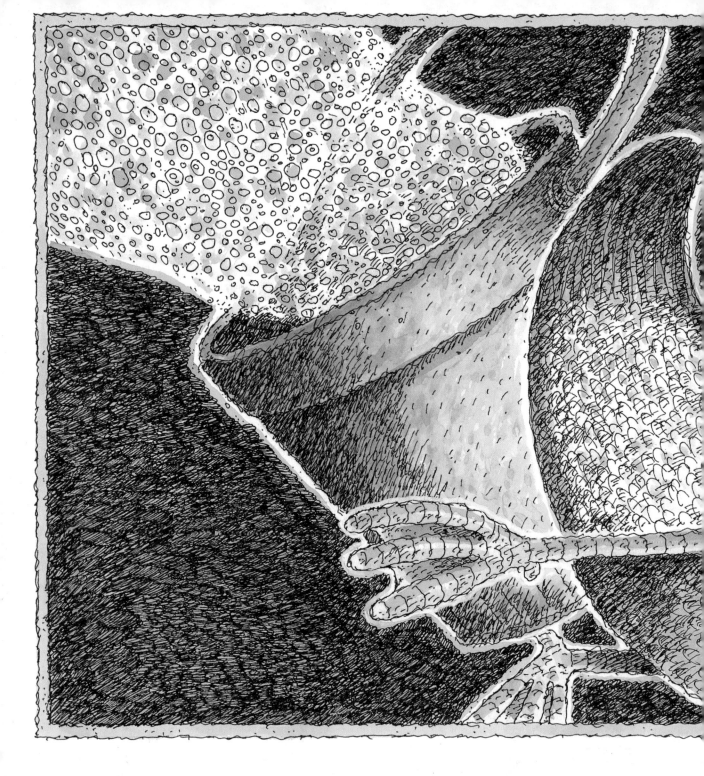

She swallowed the sand to fill up the pail.

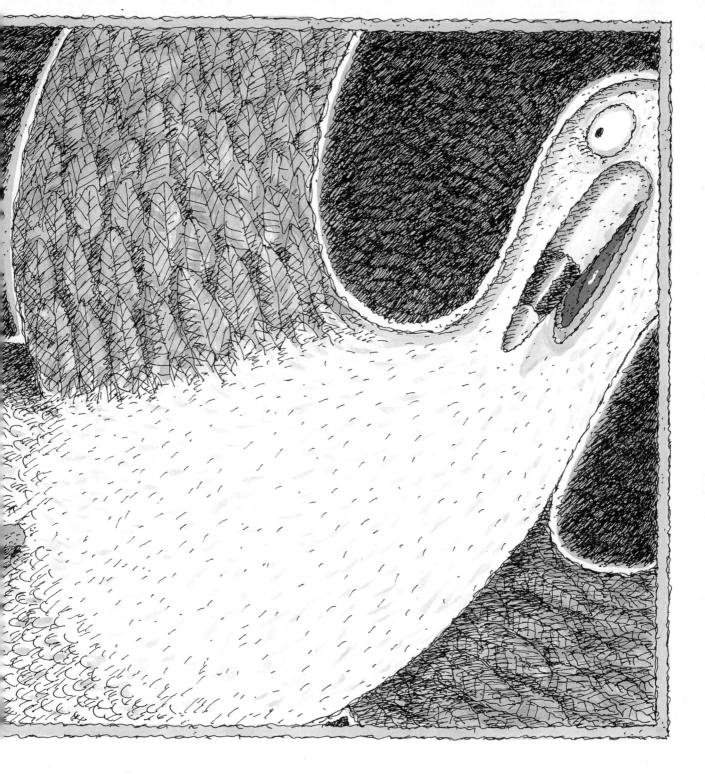

She swallowed the pail to carry the gull.

She swallowed the gull to scoop up the fish.

She swallowed the fish to catch the crab.

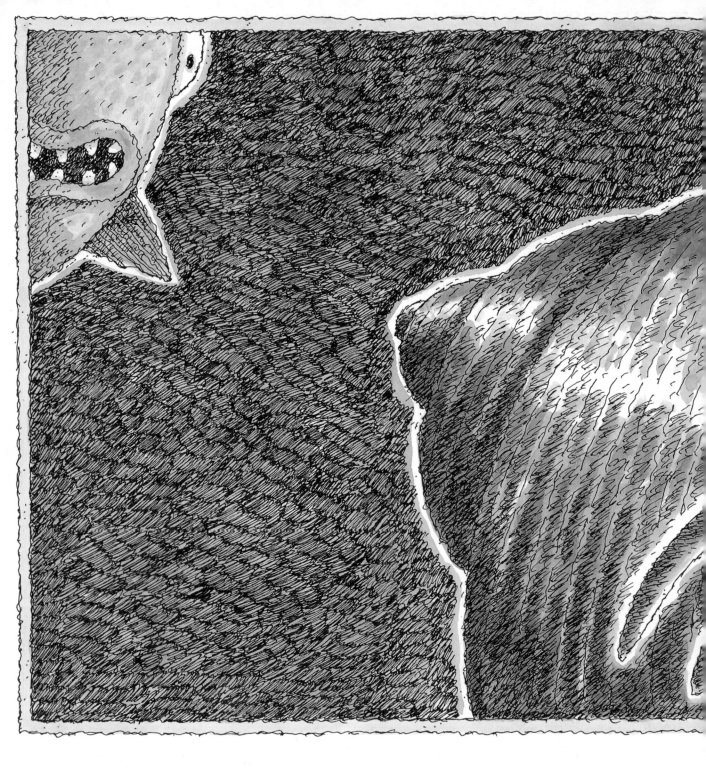

She swallowed the crab to live in the shell.

But I don't know why she swallowed the shell.
She didn't tell.

There was an old lady who swallowed a wave.

Swallowing a wave was such a big hassle,

that she suddenly burped . . .

and built a sand castle!